Paddington's

FIRST WORD BOOK

hat

basket

eggs

hen

grass

chicks

Michael Bond
Illustrated by John Lobban

PUFFIN BOOKS

PUFFIN BOOKS
Published by the Penguin Group
Penguin Putnam Inc., 375 Hudson Street, New York, New York 10014, U.S.A.
Penguin Books Ltd, 27 Wrights Lane, London W8 5TZ, England
Penguin Books Australia Ltd, Ringwood, Victoria, Australia
Penguin Books Canada Ltd, 10 Alcorn Avenue, Toronto, Ontario, Canada M4V 3B2
Penguin Books (N.Z.) Ltd, 182-190 Wairau Road, Auckland 10, New Zealand

Penguin Books Ltd, Registered Offices: Harmondsworth, Middlesex, England

First published in Great Britain by HarperCollins Publishers Ltd, 1993
First published in the United States of America by Puffin Books,
a member of Penguin Putnam Inc., 1998

1 3 5 7 9 10 8 6 4 2

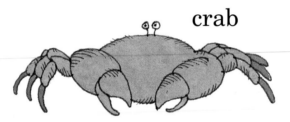

crab

Contents

pig

Paddington at the Station

Paddington Bear traveled from Peru to England not knowing where he would live. Mr. and Mrs. Brown found him and invited him to live with them.

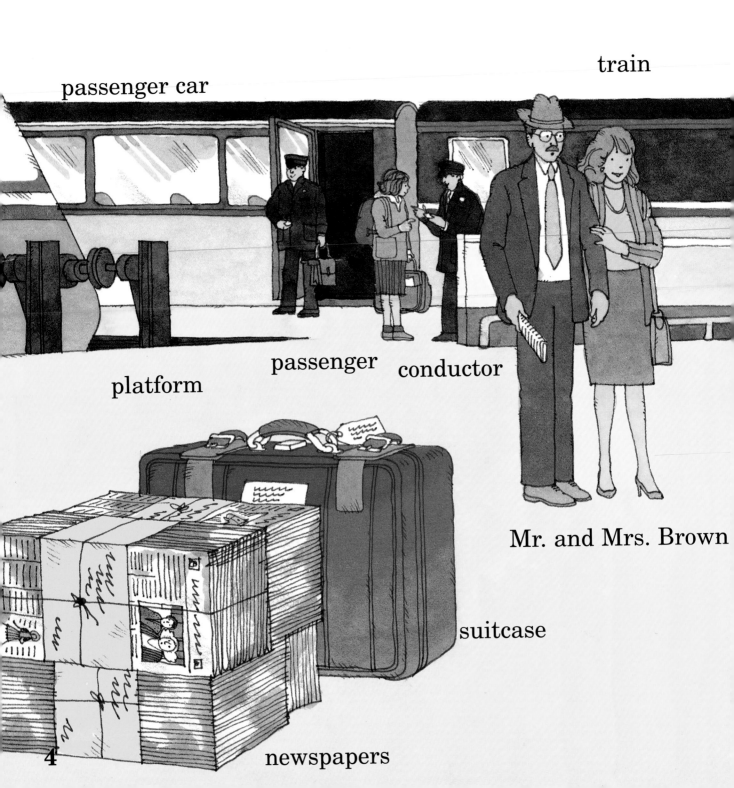

passenger car

train

platform

passenger

conductor

Mr. and Mrs. Brown

suitcase

4

newspapers

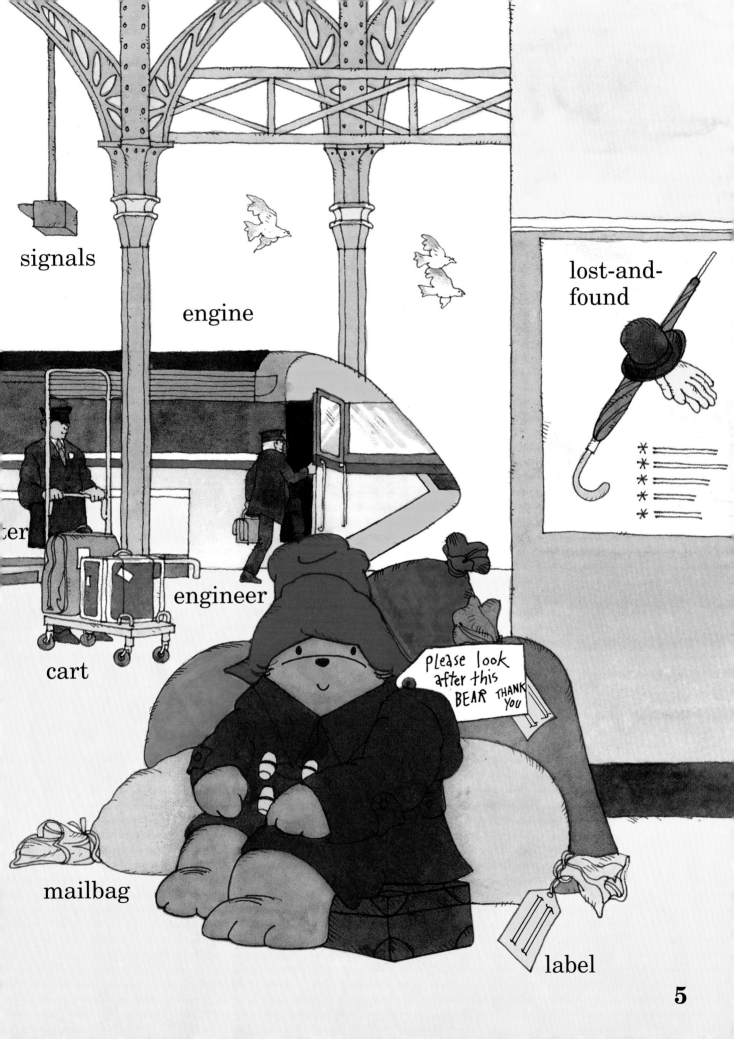

signals

engine

lost-and-found

cart

engineer

Please look after this BEAR THANK YOU

mailbag

label

5

roof

house

window

tree

door

bushes

32

steps

wall

6

A New Home for Paddington

Mr. and Mrs. Brown and Judy took Paddington home to 32 Windsor Gardens. Mrs. Bird opened the door to welcome them home.

garage

lamppost

gate

sidewalk

Paddington's Bedroom

When Paddington woke up after his first night in his new home, he discovered that he had a room to himself—and breakfast in bed.

bed

lamp

pillow

cup

plate

hairbrush

tray

sheet

blanket

picture

mirror

curtains

night table

closet

rain
boots

drawer

9

A Shopping Trip

Mrs. Brown, Judy, and Jonathan decided to take Paddington on a shopping trip. Their first stop was the supermarket.

customer

money

cart

cash register

bread

floor

baskets

bananas

carrots

cabbage

scale

bottles

cans

shelves

marmalade

oranges

11

Learning to Cook

Paddington wanted to surprise everyone by making a cake. Unfortunately, baking was not as simple as it looked.

saucepan

butter

oven

table

flour

egg
cart

kettle

ashing machine

refrigerator

wooden
spoon

ng bowl

broom

egg

stool

dustpan

13

coat hooks

drawing

door

student

chair

paintbrus

painting

paper

des

14

Going to School

Paddington was always very curious about what children do at school, and one day he went to see for himself.

teacher

blackboard

map

$6 \times 3 =$

$2 \times 7 =$

pencil

note-book

paint

trash

bage

chalk

A Day at the Beach

Paddington's visit to the beach was a special treat that he greatly enjoyed.

seagull

wave

shovel

beach ball

sand castle

bucket

shell

rock

inner tube

seaweed

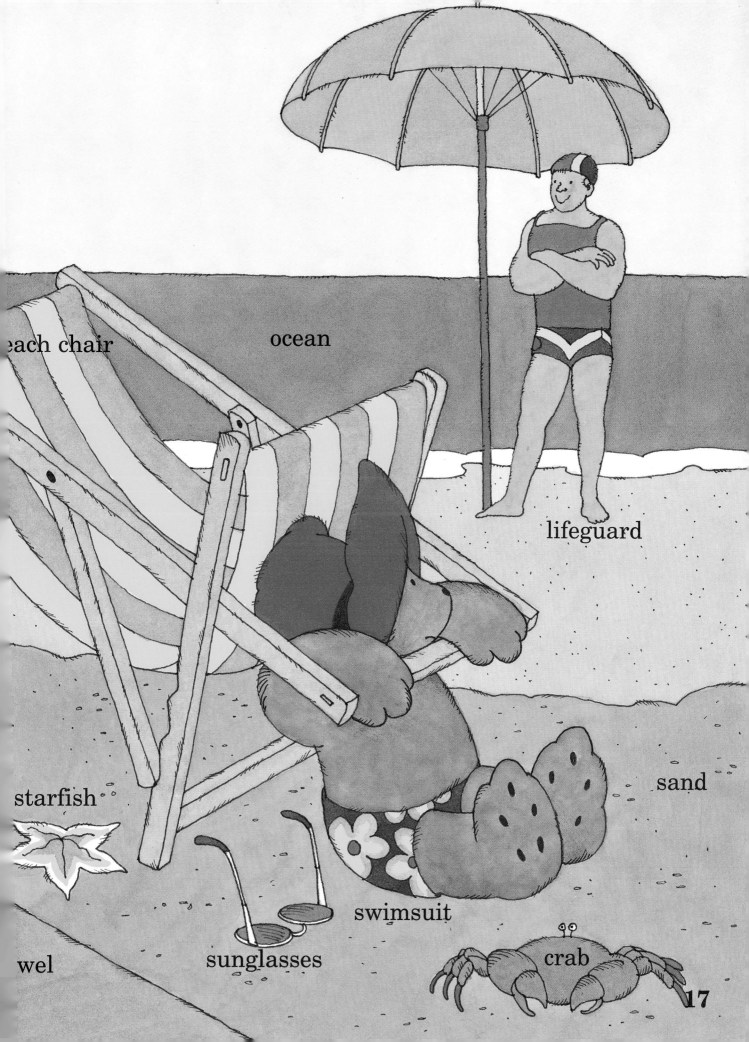

each chair

ocean

lifeguard

starfish

sand

wel

sunglasses

swimsuit

crab

17

Down on the Farm

On another outing, Paddington spent a day on a farm.

barn

stable

horses

tractor

cat

lamb

goose

rooster

farmhouse

field

sheep

pig

cow

basket

eggs

hen

egg

chicks

19

trapeze

tent

trapeze
artist

bicycle

clow

elephant

At the Circus

One day Mr. Brown treated the whole family to a
visit to the circus.

top hat

band

juggler

balloons

stilts

ringmaster

hat

21

kite

tree

ball

flower bed

ice cream

grass

lake

22

duck

bush

picnic basket

swing

baby carriage

dog

sandwiches

blanket

A Picnic in the Park

The Browns live near Hyde Park. One day they all went for a picnic by the lake.

23

Gardening

One of the things Paddington enjoys about living with the Browns is looking after the garden.

robin

fence

rock garden

flowerpot

flowers

trowel

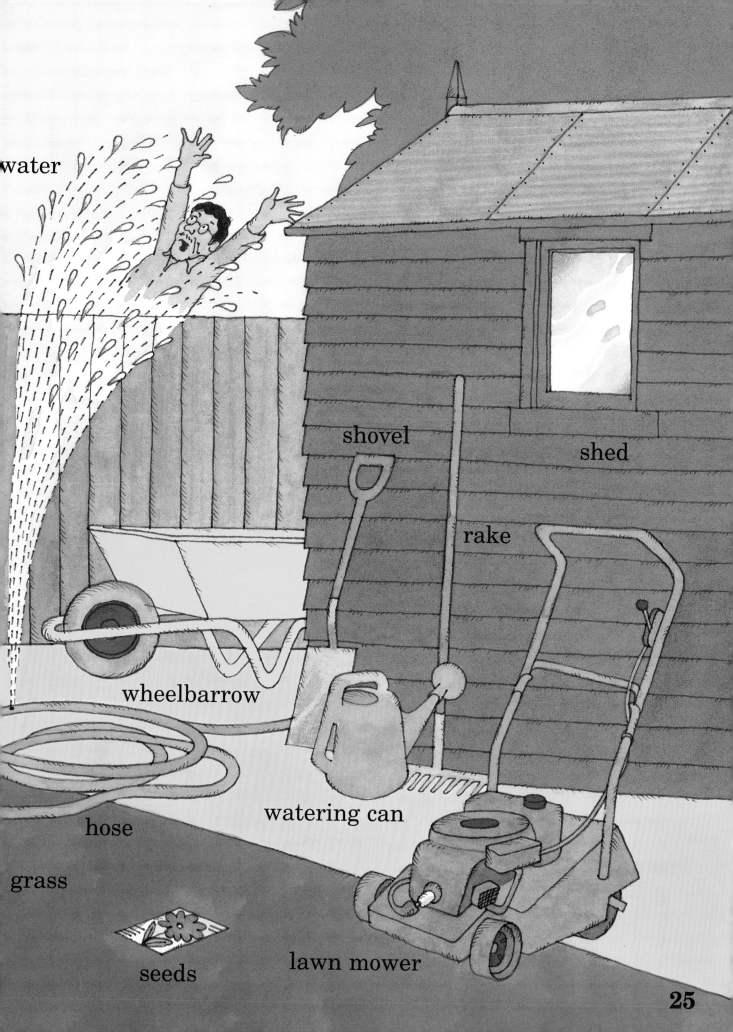

water

shovel

shed

rake

wheelbarrow

watering can

hose

grass

seeds

lawn mower

Winter Sports

Paddington wasn't too sure that he wanted to try his paw at skiing.

lodge

skier

ski suit

snow

ice ska

A Party for Paddington

At Paddington's birthday party, he thought he would entertain the guests himself.

lamp

armchair

plant

tablecloth

hammer

bookcase

magic
wand

top hat

stopwatch

sofa

rabbit

cloak

handkerchief

marmalade sandwich

29

Word List

match these pictures with the right words?

cabbage
garbage can
sled
flowerpot

window
saucepan
seagull
hammer

balloons
sandwiches
newspapers
cow